P Munsc

Munsch, R.
So much snow!

3593/sn)

SEP 1 5 2016

W9-DGK-156

SO MUCH SNOW!

Robert Munsch

illustrated by
Michael Martchenko

North Winds Press
An Imprint of Scholastic Canada Ltd.

Library and Archives Canada Cataloguing in Publication

Munsch, Robert N., 1945-, author
So much snow! / Robert Munsch ; illustrated by Michael
Martchenko.

ISBN 978-1-4431-4616-6 (hardback)

I. Martchenko, Michael, illustrator II. Title.

PS8576.U575S58 2016   jC813'.54   C2016-902570-5

www.scholastic.ca

The art for this book was painted in watercolour on Crescent illustration board.
The type is set in 21 point Barcelona ITC Std.

6 5 4 3 2 1   Printed in Canada   119   16 17 18 19 20

For Jasmine Moran,
Lockport, New York.
— R.M.

"A blizzard! A blizzard! A blizzard!" said Jasmine's mother. "Maybe you should not go to school today."

"There is no snow *now*," said Jasmine. "And besides, I like snow. I want to go to school. It's Pizza Day."

"Dress really warm," said her mother.

So Jasmine dressed really warm. Right away, it started to snow very hard.

Jasmine sang:

"Neat! Neat! Snowy feet!
Snowy feet can't be beat.
Neat! Neat! Snowy feet!
Snowy feet can't be beat.
Wintertime is fun!"

Jasmine walked down the road toward the school. By the time she got to the corner, the snow was up to her knees.

Jasmine sang:

"Gee! Gee! Frozen knees!
Boots are filling up on me.
Gee! Gee! Frozen knees!
Boots are filling up on me.
Wintertime is fun!"

Jasmine walked and walked and walked, and soon the snow was up to her bum.

Jasmine sang:

"Poor bum! Frozen numb!
Snow's so deep, I can't run.
Poor bum! Frozen numb!
Snow's so deep, I can't run.
Wintertime is fun."

Jasmine walked and walked and walked. She could see the school, but the snow was up to her nose. Jasmine sang:

"Oh no, it's at my nose!
What if the whole world froze?
Oh no, it's at my nose!
What if the whole world froze?
Wintertime is fun?"

Jasmine stopped walking and
the snow kept coming down and
soon only the top of her hat was
above the snow.
Jasmine sang:

"Oh, dread! Over my head!
I wish I was home in bed!
Oh, dread! Over my head!
I wish I was home in bed!
Wintertime's no fun."

She stood there singing for a long time. Finally the school caretaker came stomping through the snow on a pair of snowshoes.

He pulled up Jasmine by her hat and yelled, "AHHHHHHHHHHH! Frozen kid!"

Then he went stomping back through the blizzard, pulling Jasmine behind him.

"Where are we going?" said Jasmine.

"I'm taking you to the nurse's office," said the caretaker. "We will get you warmed up and if you are OK, I will take you to your classroom."

So he took Jasmine inside to the nurse's office and dropped her onto a chair.

The vice principal came in and said, "You're frozen stiff! Let's get you warmed up. Here are some nice blankets."

She wrapped Jasmine in ten layers of blankets, but Jasmine did not unfreeze.

The school secretary came in and said, "You're frozen stiff! Let's get you warmed up. I will go get you a nice cup of hot chocolate."

She poured the hot chocolate into Jasmine's mouth.

"Yum!" said Jasmine, but she did not unfreeze.

Finally the caretaker came back.
He took one look at Jasmine and said,
"You're still frozen? Let me see what I
can do."

He got a huge duster and tickled
Jasmine under the chin.

Jasmine started to laugh and

CRACK!

the ice shattered into a million pieces.

So the caretaker took her to her class. On the way there they went past the principal's office.

"Hey," said the principal, "what are you two doing here? There's a blizzard outside and it is not going to stop, so we are having a snow day! Everyone has to go home!"

"Wait a minute!" said Jasmine. "It's Pizza Day!"

27

So they all went out for lunch
and Jasmine sang:

"Snowing a little or snowing a lot,
Winter's OK when you've got
Help to get you through bad spots.
Wintertime is fun!"